PUFFIN BOOKS

TALE OF A ONE-WAY STREET
and other stories

Strange and wonderful things happen when this book is opened: Gus can remember amazing things that never happened (like being given a zebra for his birthday) when he holds a leaf from the memory tree in his hand; Tansy discovers that the moon is covered in daisies; Bridget rescues the king of grasshoppers from a steaming bowl of porridge and is given a fabulous reward; and Soapy Sam tries to steal his mother's charmed Goodbye Song, with disastrous results!

These are just a few of Joan Aiken's original stories of imagination, which take us to peculiar lands where dreams and wishes can come true. Each story is beautifully illustrated by Jan Pieńkowski's delicate silhouettes, making this superb collection one which any child will treasure.

Joan Aiken's previous books in Puffin include *A Necklace of Raindrops* and *The Kingdom Under the Sea*, both illustrated by Jan Pieńkowski.

D0431656

JOAN AIKEN

Tale of a One-Way Street

AND OTHER STORIES

pictures by
JAN PIEŃKOWSKI

PUFFIN BOOKS

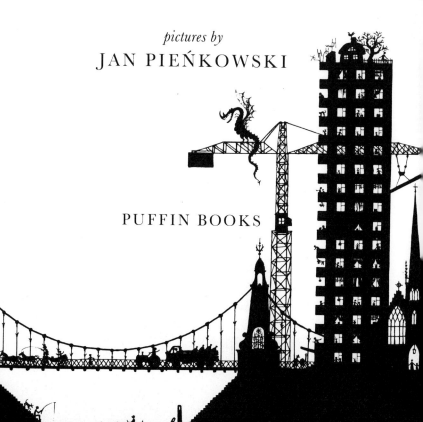

Puffin Books, Penguin Books Ltd, Harmondsworth, Middlesex, England
Penguin Books, 40 West 23rd Street, New York, New York 10010, U.S.A.
Penguin Books Australia Ltd, Ringwood, Victoria, Australia
Penguin Books Canada Ltd, 2801 John Street, Markham, Ontario, Canada L3R 1B4
Penguin Books (N.Z.) Ltd, 182–190 Wairau Road, Auckland 10, New Zealand

First published by Jonathan Cape Ltd 1978
Published in Puffin Books 1984
'Bridget's Hat' and 'Clean Sheets' first appeared in *Puffin Post*

The illustrator would like to thank his godchildren:
Kate Dixon, Loveday Gibbons, Rufus Howell, Selina Lyon
and Jemima Gibbons for their assistance in painting
the picture on page 19

Made and printed in Hong Kong
Set in Monotype Baskerville

Tale
of a
One-Way
Street

and other stories

Contents

From Joan
to EUAN CUNNINGHAM

From Jan
to DAVID WALSER

Tale of a
One-Way Street

There was a little town which had a one-way street in it. In this town also, the postman carried a walkie-talkie radio set, so that as he went along the streets, putting people's letters through their front doors, he could report all the news back to the post office.

"Mrs Jones got a postcard from her son in Rome. And she's having fried eggs for breakfast."

"Mr Smith's parcel of fish-hooks has come at last. But one of his front windows is broken; it looked as if a bird had flown into it."

"Miss Brown's mother in Ipswich sent her a currant cake. Very good; she just gave me a piece. And her white cat has had kittens in front of the kitchen fire: two, at present."

The people in the post office, who had to spend all day sorting letters into little heaps, one heap for each street, were very pleased to get all this interesting news while they did their dull job.

One morning the postman said,

"I'm at the top of the one-way street. There's a mover's van halfway down the hill. I reckon a new family is moving into the empty house. I'll tell you more later."

And he started down the one-way street, putting letters through people's letter-boxes as he went along.

The name of this street was really Narrow Hill. Because it was so narrow, and so steep, the traffic was only allowed to go down it, never up, and so everyone in the town had fallen into the habit of calling it the one-way street, instead of using its proper name.

"Good morning," said the postman to the new family who were moving their furniture out of the van. "Any letters for you, I wonder?"

"Mann, the name is," said the father. "Mr and Mrs Mann. And young Tom Mann."

"Number Fifty, Mr and Mrs Mann," said the postman writing it down.

"No letters today, but perhaps there'll be some tomorrow."

Mr Mann stuck up a sign that said, T. MANN, PLUMBER. Mrs Mann carried in a last load of sheets and towels. Then the mover's van drove off.

When young Tom Mann put his head out of the front door, after helping to carry in all the furniture, a thrush flying past overhead called,

"Hullo, young Tom Mann! You must turn right!"

And a horse trotting past, pulling a cart full of beer barrels, called,

"Turn right, Tom Mann, turn right, clippety-clop, turn right."

"Why must I turn right?" said Tom. "If I turn right, that takes me down to the bottom of the hill. But I want to go up to the top."

"You must turn right because it is a one-way street," said the postman, walking on down the hill, putting letters into people's boxes.

"Good morning, I'm the postman with
one-way feet,
And I walk one way along the one-way
street."

The thrush, flying overhead, called,
"I'm the bird that nests in your garden
and sings,
And I fly along the one-way street on
one-way wings."
A boy riding past on his bike shouted,
"I'm Bill, with a bike with a brake that
squeals,
I bike along the one-way street on one-
way wheels."
A girl skated down the road on roller-skates,
calling as she went,
"I'm Susan, a girl who never stands and
waits,
I skate along the one-way street on one-
way skates."
A coal-man with a lorry delivering coal called
down from his driver's cab,
"I'm the coal-man who carries in the coal
for your fires,
I drive along the one-way street on one-
way tyres."

A cat, hurrying along the garden walls, stopped
to say,
 "I catch nice mice in my clever claws,
 And I trot along the one-way street on
 one-way paws."
A gull called down from high up,
 "I float one way over all the roofs,"
and the horse, pulling his beer cart, neighed,
 "I canter one way on my one-way hoofs."
 And the sun, high overhead in the sky, winked
its great golden eye as a cloud sailed past under-
neath, and said,
 "I'm the sun who shines in the sky so bright,
 I travel one way from morning to night."

"But what happens if I want to go the other way?" said Tom.

"You'd get run over and squashed flat," said the postman.

"All the birds would bump into you," said the thrush.

"So would the horses," said the horse.

"You'd get lost and never come home again," said Bill and Susan.

"Nobody ever *has* gone the other way," said the coal-man. "It's not allowed."

"I don't see why," said Tom, but at that moment his mother put her head out of the front door and said, "Tom, it's time for dinner, and don't let me hear any talk about your going the wrong way along the one-way street. Why, goodness knows where you'd end up! At the North Pole, most likely!"

So Tom went in to dinner, and all the other people went their way down the hill, skating or walking or driving or biking or flying or trotting.

But Tom kept thinking about the one-way street as he ate his boiled egg. Boiled eggs and bread-and-butter was what they had for lunch, because of having just moved into the house. Mrs Mann had not had time to get to the shops yet.

"Mother," said Tom, "how do you boil an egg?"

"There's only one way to boil an egg properly," said his mother.

"You put it into boiling water and wait till it's done.

> You could keep on boiling eggs all day,
> But still there's only one right way."

"And how do you make bread and butter?" said Tom.

"There's only one way. You put the butter on the bread and spread it.

> Take loaf, take butter, and cut, and spread,
> There's only one way to put butter on bread."

"How do you mend a burst pipe?" Tom asked his father.

"There's nobbut one way to do it properly," said Tom's father, and he told Tom how it was done.

> "Smooth and solder and work and wipe,
> There's only one way to mend a pipe."

Tom listened to his father and his mother, and he said to himself,

"I can see there's only one way to boil an egg and spread butter and mend a pipe, but there are *two* ways to walk along a street, and I don't see why I'm not allowed to use them both."

But he didn't say this out loud. His mother was busy moving tables and chairs around, to see which way looked best, and his father was hard at work, deciding which things ought to go into which rooms.

Tom went and looked out through the front window at the one-way street. Every moving thing that he could see was going *down* the hill—cars and carts, prams and bikes, ladies and dogs and pushchairs and bakers' vans.

"Just the same," thought Tom, "some day I am going *up* that hill, to find out where it goes."

Next day Tom went down the hill to school at the bottom. And there he learned to read.

"There's only one way to learn reading," said the teacher. "You have to start with letters.

There's just one way and that is that

c-a-t spells nothing but cat."

Next Tom learned sums.

"There's only one way, there aren't any more

Two plus two makes only four."

On his way home from school Tom thought harder than ever about the one-way street. He had to go home a different way, which took longer, along Traders' Lane, and Market Hill, and Church Walk, and Parson's Steps, which brought him out at the top of Narrow Hill, and then he could run down the street to his home.

Each day at school the lessons were just the same, until they came to Friday. On Friday they had painting, and the painting teacher was somebody new, somebody Tom had not seen before.

When Tom asked,

"What is the proper way to paint a picture?" this teacher said,

"There isn't any right way. There are hundreds of ways, and each one is different. You just have to take your courage in your hands and begin."

Tom didn't know how to take his courage in his hands, but he took paper and brushes and paints, and he painted a picture of Narrow Hill, the one-way street, with the houses going right up the hill and off the top of the paper.

Susan looked over his shoulder and said, "You silly boy! There ought to be *sky* at the top, not houses. And who ever heard of a *pink cat*?"

Bill looked over his shoulder and said, "All the things in your picture are going the wrong way, if that is meant to be our street. And I never yet saw a dark-blue horse. You must be crazy!"

But the teacher looked at Tom's picture and said,

"You keep on exploring that avenue, boy, and you may find out a secret or two, by and by."

Tom was surprised, because he thought his picture was of a street, not an avenue, but he was pleased when the teacher put it up on the wall and stuck a gold star on it.

Next morning was Saturday, so there was no school. It was a quiet, foggy, misty, grey, empty day which seemed to have no beginning or middle or end. The sun didn't even try to shine through the fog. Tom's mother was painting the bathroom walls, and his father was fixing the kitchen taps, both very busy, so Tom thought,

"Now is my chance."

He put on his long woolly scarf, and he took his courage in both hands, now that he knew how, and he went out of the front door and turned left up the hill, into the thick, white, woolly fog. It was very queer, rather like being inside a white parcel, and at first Tom didn't much care for it.

But then he heard a pit-a-pat noise, and he saw a bright pink cat trotting along just ahead of him.

"Hullo, young Tom Mann," said the cat. "Going my way?"

"Yes, I think so, thank you," said Tom, and he followed the pink cat.

Now beyond the pink cat he noticed a yellow seagull and a silver thrush, flying through the mist.

"Hullo, Tom," they called. "Are you going our way?"

"Yes, I believe so, thank you," said Tom.

Next he saw a pea-green postman with a sack of mail, and a bright red coal-man, whose lorry was stacked with scarlet bags of coal.

"Good morning, Tom," they said. "Going our way, are you?"

"Yes, thank you," said Tom. And then he saw a dark-blue horse, and a golden girl on roller-skates, and an orange boy on a bike.

"Hi there, Tom," they called. "Are you going our way?"

"Yes I am," said Tom.

Then he came to the top of the hill. There was the sun, standing still overhead and shining bright violet rays down across the country on the other side of the hill. The fog stopped here like a wall. Tom, and all the people with him, could see for miles and miles into the land that lay beyond, but they could not see right across, because the country was far too wide.

What they could see was very surprising.

They saw a whole mountain of boiled eggs, each one different from all the others. They saw a whole field paved with slices of bread-and-butter, no two of them alike. They saw a great forest of pipes, each pipe mended in a different way. They saw streams and fountains of letters and numbers sparkling in the purple rays of the sun, making hundreds and thousands of different words, giving the answers to any number of sums. And all the words were right, and all were different. All the sums were right and all were different.

In the middle, on a sunny hillside, under a tree covered in cherries the size of apples, or apples the colour of cherries, was a comfortable chair with a label on it that said TOM.

"Now I know," said Tom, to the cat and the gull and the thrush and the postman and the coal-man and the horse and the boy and the girl, "that while I thought I was coming your way, *you* were all coming *my* way. And now I know about

this place, I shall come here as often as I like."

He sat down comfortably in the chair and watched three lemon-yellow fish jumping in the fountain, catching the numbers in their mouths.

The cat chased a pink mouse, the postman delivered half a dozen pea-green letters, and the dark-blue horse nibbled a clump of red primroses.

When Tom went home, he found his mother still painting the bathroom and his father still fixing the kitchen taps. Neither of them had noticed that he had been gone.

"Oh, Tom," said his mother. "Run down the hill, will you, and buy me a bottle of Jollyclens, that's the only stuff to get paint off paintbrushes."

"And while you're at it," said his father, "get me a packet of Smith's Superfine Staples. Don't get any other kind."

"Okay," said Tom, and he took the money his mother gave him and went out of the front door, turning right and running down the steep hill, going the same way as all the cars and horses and prams and bikes and vans and ladies with their dogs. For now the fog had lifted and he could see everything as plain as plain.

He bought the Jollyclens and the Smith's Superfine Staples, and went back, taking the way he came after school, by Traders' Lane, and Market Hill, and Church Walk, and Parson's Steps, and so to the top of Narrow Hill, from where he could run all the way to his front door. And as he ran he sang,

"I'm Tom, the boy with one-way feet
And I run one way along the one-way
street."

When he got home he gave his mother the bottle of Jollyclens and he said to her,

"Mum."

"Well?"

"You *can't* walk more than one way at a time, can you?"

"Of course you can't," said his mother. "Don't be silly. And go and put on the kettle for tea. I've made a very nice new kind of cake. It's on the shelf in the larder."

The postman, on his walkie-talkie set, reported back to the post office,

"The new family, halfway up Narrow Hill, seems to be settling in nicely."

The Lions

In the middle of a town by a river there was once a little park, not much bigger than somebody's front garden. It was all paved with brick, and in the centre of it grew a weeping willow tree. Around the edge of the garden stood a row of red geraniums in pots. Along one side, beyond a white railing, flowed the green river, breaking into foamy ripples and waves in its hurry, sometimes throwing up sudden bursts of bubbles. And at each corner of the little park, facing inwards so that they could see one another comfortably, crouched four stone lions. One had moss growing on his tail. One had a swallow's nest of straw built between his ears. One had a broken paw, where a boy had thrown a brick. And somebody had written I LOVE FRANK on the fourth lion. But the word FRANK, down by his tail, had been nearly washed off by rain, and the word I was tangled up in his mane, so that if you glanced quickly, the lion seemed to have been labelled LOVE.

The four lions talked to each other all day long, without making a sound.

Over on the other side of the green rushing river was a huge rubbish dump; all the empty tins, broken bottles, old bones, torn newspapers and boxes, rotten vegetables, worn-out clothes, radio sets and shoes, damaged chairs, smashed plates, dead flowers, fish-heads, and unpaid bills that people in the town wanted to throw away, they rowed in boats across the river, or carried over the bridge, and flung on to this heap, which was now higher than any church in the town. When the sun was low the shadow of the heap stretched right over the water.

The lions had a friend who visited them in their garden every day. In fact they had two friends. Each afternoon an old man in a wheel-chair was brought there by his daughter, who left him for a couple of hours while she did her shopping. If the weather was fine, she left his chair close by the railing where he could most easily hear the river, for he was rather deaf. But if it rained, or was likely to, she left him under the weeping willow, which was even better than an umbrella.

The old man carried his canary with him, in a cage on his knee. Every day, the minute his daughter was out of sight, he opened the cage door and let the canary fly out. First it shot up into the willow tree with a burst of song; then it would fly to the railing and look at the river; then it would visit the lions, each in turn, and take them the old man's greetings. For the canary could listen to the old man's thoughts, and translate them into song; and it could also hear what the lions were thinking and carry their silent speech to the old man. So every day these friends would have a long, interesting conversation. Sometimes the old man told the lions about his life. He had been a sailor when he was younger, travelling all over the world. And the lions had had many adventures too, for long ago, before they had been brought to their present place, they had kept guard over the tomb of a great king in a desert land, many thousands of miles away, and for hundreds of years they had watched over the comings and goings of priests and noblemen and common people coming to pay their respects at the tomb. So there was always plenty to talk about, and the canary flew to and fro, making a pattern like a yellow star as it flashed from one corner of the garden to another, and back to the tree in the middle, taking a question or a joke or a thought from one friend to another as if it carried a bundle of words on its yellow back.

One day the old man was rather late.

"What can be keeping him?" said the moss-tailed lion.

"The sun is behind the church spire already," said the straw-capped lion.

"The old man has been rather pale these last few days," said the lion with the broken paw.

"Perhaps he is ill," said the lion labelled LOVE.

"How long has he been coming to our garden?" said Moss Tail.

"Only since they built the new bridge," said Straw Cap. "Thirty winters, no more."

"A long time in men's counting," said Broken Paw.

"Here he comes now," said Love.

The old man's daughter wheeled him in and left him under the weeping willow, for the sky was grey. Today the old man was wrapped in a thick rug.

"Are you sure you will be all right, Father?" said the daughter. "Will you be warm enough?"

"Yes, thank you, my dear."

"I'll be back soon. I'll be as quick as I can."

"Don't worry. Enjoy your shopping. I like to sit here," he said, as she hurried away. And he opened the cage door and let out the canary, who darted like a yellow flash of sunshine to each lion in turn.

"The old man is not very well today," he told them. "I'm afraid that in the winter he won't be able to come to the garden any more."

The lions were dismayed.

"How shall we be able to have our conversations? We shall miss him," said Moss Tail.

"Can you fly to us from his house?" said Straw Cap.

"No, for his daughter won't let me out. She is afraid that I might be stolen, or get lost," said the bird.

"Perhaps the old man can persuade her," said

Broken Paw.

"But if he is
ill, the canary
should stay
with him,"
said Love.

"Let us not
waste time
worrying about
the winter,"
said the old man.
"Let us talk
while we can,
and finish as
much as possible
of what we have
to say."

"What shall we
talk about today?"
said Moss Tail.

"The rubbish dump,"
said Straw Cap.

"Yes, we should
certainly talk about
that," said Broken Paw.
"Today its shadow
almost reaches across the
river."

"What can be done
about it?" said Moss Tail.

"I have a suggestion," said Love. "Let me think about it a little longer so as to get it quite clear in my head."

"Do you suppose people have made rubbish heaps like that all over the world?" said Straw Cap to the old man.

"Most probably," he said.

"Then we should talk about them all," said Broken Paw. "What is your idea, Love?"

During this time the canary had been busily flying back and forth between the lions and the old man, rather like a spider spinning a web. Now, as the lion called Love was still not quite ready to explain his idea, the canary took a rest for a moment, perching on the railing by the river.

At this moment a man came rowing down the river. He had unloaded a whole boatful of broken television sets on to the rubbish dump and jumped

back into his empty boat. Then, spying the canary, as a current carried him to that side of the river, he pulled a big red handkerchief out of his pocket, flung it over the bird, stuffed handkerchief, bird and all into a wicker basket he had in the boat, and was away down the river before either the old man or the lions realised what was happening.

Indeed the old man, who was very short-sighted, did not know that his canary had been stolen; he sat patiently waiting, expecting that in a moment or two the little bird would fly back to him with some thought from one of the lions.

The lions were terribly upset.

"Our translator has been kidnapped," said Moss Tail.

"What shall we do?" said Straw Cap.

"We'll never be able to get him back," said Broken Paw.

"But we must try to," said Love.

"Without him we can't talk to the old man," said Moss Tail.

"And he can't talk to us," said Straw Cap.

"We shall never be able to put our heads together and make a plan to get rid of the rubbish heap," said Broken Paw.

"We need help," said Love.

"What is happening?" said the old man. "Why does nobody speak?"

"You can't hear us," said Moss Tail.

"Oh, this is dreadfully sad," said Straw Cap,

and a stone tear as big as a tennis ball rolled down his nose and on to his paws.

"I don't see how we can be helped," said Broken Paw.

But Love called up to a golden eagle flying overhead.

"Can you see a man in a boat with a basket? Is he still on the river?"

"Yes, I can see him," said the golden eagle, hovering far up in the sunshine on his powerful wings. "Why do you want to know? He is going down the river, heading for the sea."

"He has made off with a friend of ours, a canary," said Moss Tail.

"How can we prevent him getting away?" said Straw Cap.

"You could sink his boat," said the golden eagle, swooping down to perch on the fence.

"How?" said Straw Cap.

"Drop something heavy on it," said the golden eagle. "I could easily overtake the boat and drop a heavy weight on it, if you can give me something suitable."

"But what do we have?" said Moss Tail.

"My tear?" said Straw Cap.

"Not heavy enough," said the golden eagle, after he had picked up the tear to test it.

"We have nothing else," said Broken Paw. "We have lost our only chance."

"We have ourselves," said Love.

"One of *us*?" said Moss Tail.

"But," said Broken Paw, "which ever one of us the golden eagle dropped would end up at the bottom of the river."

"We are made of stone. Whoever it was would come to no harm," said Love.

"It would be lonely down there," said Moss Tail.

"How would he get back?" said Straw Cap.

"He might be down there for a hundred years," said Broken Paw.

"We have no choice," said Love.

"Why does nobody speak to me?" said the old man.

"We must hurry and do *something*," said Moss Tail.

"Oh, this is terrible," said Broken Paw, and he too dropped a stone tear.

"You'll have to be quick making up your minds," said the golden eagle. "The boat is getting very close to the sea."

"Which of us shall it be?" said Love.

"I can't go because of the swallows nesting

between my ears," said Straw Cap.

"I might not be heavy enough, with my broken paw," said Broken Paw.

"I haven't the courage," said Moss Tail.

"Then I had better go," said Love.

So the golden eagle flew to Love, and took a firm grip with his powerful claws on the lion's mane and tail.

He flapped his great wings and rose into the air, more slowly than usual, for Love was a massive weight, carved from pure marble.

"Goodbye," called Moss Tail sadly.

"Goodbye," called Broken Paw.

"Goodbye," called Straw Cap.

"Perhaps we shall see each other again," said

Love. Then the golden eagle dropped Love, who fell like a thunderbolt, smashing clean through the boat and sinking it instantly. And the thief was carried down with it and drowned.

But the golden eagle dived, almost as fast as Love fell, and snatched up the wicker basket which remained floating on the water. He flew back and laid the basket on the lap of the old man, who was very much surprised. He felt for the catch and let out the canary.

"Why, what has been happening to you, my poor bird?"

"Oh, sir!" said the canary. "I have had such a narrow escape! A man in a boat grabbed me in a red cloth, and if, by some strange piece of luck, the boat had not sunk, and if, by some mysterious stroke of fortune, an eagle had not kindly picked me up, I should never have got back to you."

"Well, and it is also very lucky that my daughter has not returned yet," said the old man. "For she is always saying that if I let you fly loose, somebody might steal you.

"But now let us make haste and hear what Love has to say about the rubbish dump: he will certainly have had time to collect his thoughts by now."

However, just at that moment, the old man's daughter did come back, so the canary hurriedly hopped into his cage, the old man snapped the catch, and the daughter wheeled the pair of them

away so fast that they did not realise one lion was gone; the canary was too flustered and the old man was too short-sighted.

"Will they come back tomorrow, do you think?" said Straw Cap.

"I wonder if we shall ever see Love again," said Broken Paw.

After that there was silence in the garden for a long time, while each of the three thought his own thoughts, and the river rushed by.

And below the rushing green water, deep down on the sandy bottom at the river's mouth, Love lay motionless, with his head on his paws, patiently waiting until somebody should come to rescue him.

Bridget's Hat

Once a twin brother and sister called Solomon and Bridget lived together in a little tumbledown house on the edge of a town. Bridget worked hard to earn their food by sewing: she made dresses and hats, petticoats and curtains, shirts and skirts and babies' clothes for all the ladies of the town. Solomon never did anything; he lay out in the long grass at the back of their little house all day long, sunning himself and snoozing, snoring when he was asleep, alternately singing and chewing grass-blades when he was awake. He liked to dress handsomely, so Bridget had bought him a pair of blue velvet trousers with silver studs down the seams, and a lilac-and-green shirt, and a pair of grey antelope-skin boots.

Bridget herself went barefoot, for they really had very little money, and she wore an old grey cotton dress that one of her ladies had passed on to her when it was almost worn out. But she did have a beautiful hat. The crown and the wide brim were made of sky-blue silk taffeta, cunningly banded and lapped, and decorated with a big pink velvet rose; the inside of the wide brim was all lined with grey furry moleskin; and the hat tied under her chin with two dove-grey ribbons.

Bridget had made the hat for a lady in the town whose mother died on the very day the hat was delivered.

"I shall have to wear black for at least a year," sighed the lady. "And by that time wide brims will be quite out of fashion. You had better keep the hat for yourself, Bridget, and make me a black one instead."

"What luck," said Solomon when he heard this. "You can sell that hat for a lot of money. I need some new boots; nobody wears this kind any more."

But Bridget was so fond of the hat, which had cost her hours of work, that she could not bear to sell it to anybody else; so she kept it herself and promised to save up as fast as she could for Solomon's new boots. Solomon was annoyed about this for as long as his lazy nature could be bothered, which was not more than a few weeks. After that he did not mention the matter more than once or twice a day. Bridget meant to keep the hat for best, but the wide brim was so comfortable that she wore it to shade her from the sun when she had to walk a long way from home, collecting orders or delivering dresses to her ladies. Besides, the hat was a good advertisement for her work, and suited her dark hair and blue eyes, though it did not go so well with the torn old cotton dress and bare feet.

One hot summer morning Bridget was eating her porridge on the back step of their house before walking a long way across the town to collect an order from the Queen of the land. For Bridget's stitches were so small, and her notions about colours and materials were so clever, and her prices were so low, that all the royal family employed her to make their best clothes.

She was eating her porridge fast and quietly, because her brother Solomon was still asleep inside the house, and she didn't want to wake him in case he again suggested selling her hat, when a very large grasshopper jumped slap into the middle of her porridge bowl.

"Oh dear," said Bridget, and she quickly spooned the grasshopper out of the porridge, and dipped a dipper of water from the well, and washed the grasshopper, and set him to dry in the sun.

All the other grasshoppers round about had fallen silent after the accident, but now they began chirping again. And the grasshopper she had rescued—who was indeed a very large one, quite the biggest she had ever seen—carefully waved all his legs and whiskers, and felt himself over to make sure that no stickiness remained from the porridge.

Then he turned and bowed deeply to Bridget, sweeping his whiskers right down to the ground.

"I am greatly obliged to you, my dear young lady," he said. "To drown in porridge would be a dreadfully undignified end for the King of the Grasshoppers."

"Is that what you are?" said Bridget, wondering if it would seem disrespectful to eat up the porridge that he had sat in, for she had a long walk ahead of her, and was still very hungry, and the only other food in the house was Solomon's plate of porridge.

"Certainly I am the King of the Grasshoppers. And, as a small mark of my gratitude I now intend to give you a present. What shall it be?"

"Oh my gracious," said Bridget. "Thank you, your Majesty. I really don't know what to say."

This was true; firstly because she needed so many things, and secondly because she was not sure what the grasshopper would be able to give her and did not want to hurt his feelings. Perhaps she could ask for a leaf? Or a blade of grass?

"Come, come," said the grasshopper. "What do you wish for most?"

"I wish I could jump about as quickly as your Majesty," Bridget said politely, thinking of the long hot walk through dusty tarry streets, right across to the other side of the town.

"A very good wish," said the grasshopper. "I was thinking the same thing myself, and as I see you also need a pair of shoes, we will combine the two items."

Bridget's bare feet, on the hot boards of the back steps, suddenly felt quite different, quite cool and comfortable. Looking down in surprise, she saw that she had on a pair of soft, elegant black suede boots, fitting up to the ankle; each boot was fastened with a diamond the size of a cherry.

She began to say thank you, but the grasshopper interrupted her.

"Now," he said. "Pay careful attention. The diamond that fastens your right-hand boot is a very old and precious one; it is called the Eye of the Desert, and has the power to take you wherever you want to go, if you step out with your right foot first, and wish at the same time. Is that clear? But the stone on the left boot does not have the

"Oh, my dear Bridget!" wept the Queen. "Puss is missing! We think he must have been catnapped by that wretched dragon who lives out in the desert somewhere. Not a soul has seen him since last night, he usually comes for his breakfast long before this and it was kidneys today, his favourite — and the palace baker said that when he happened to look out at dawn he saw the dragon fly past holding something black in his claws. And *nobody*

knows where the dragon has his nest, one could go on searching about that great dusty desert for years—how shall I ever get on without dear Pussums?"

"Don't worry, your Majesty," said Bridget kindly, seeing that this was no time to ask for payment for a green silk petticoat embroidered with snowdrops, "I'll have a hunt round and see if I can't find your Pussy. Perhaps things aren't as bad as you think."

She left the Queen's parlour and, stepping out into the palace courtyard on to her right foot, said,

"I wish to go where the Queen's cat is."

Although it was a hot day, the speed with which she flew across the countryside quite cooled her down. She crossed fields, woods, hills, and the burnt, brown desert.

Then she came to the foot of a cliff, which was where the dragon had his nest. There he lay, in a big round shallow hole, something like the crater of a volcano. Some birds line their nests with fluff. The dragon had lined his nest with gold coins, thick as the pebbles on a beach. In the middle was a blue, blue pool and beside it grew a huge rose-tree, all covered with pink roses. And under the rose-tree lay the dragon, fast asleep, or *almost* fast asleep, and near by, looking very sulky, but purring as loudly as possible, sat the Queen's black cat.

"What a bit of luck that the dragon didn't eat him right away; keeping him for supper, I suppose," thought Bridget, and in a whisper she called,

"Here, puss, puss, puss! Come, pussy, pussy, pussy!" for she did not wish to venture any closer to the dragon in case she woke him.

The Queen's cat stuck his tail up in the air and came galloping over to Bridget. Unfortunately he stopped purring, and this woke the dragon, for it was the sound of purring that had lulled him to sleep; directly it stopped he became fidgety.

He opened his eyes and reared his great head up into the air, so that he looked like a very large question-mark.

Bridget crouched down on the ground, thinking that her last minute had come. But because of her big blue hat, which hid her completely, the dragon, who was rather short-sighted, never saw her at all. He thought the hat was a bit of the blue pool, with a pink rose floating on it. The Queen's cat hastily started purring again and the dragon, after a sharp look all round, tucked his head under his shining wing and went back to sleep.

Bridget instantly snatched up the cat and, stepping out with her right foot, cried,

"I wish to be back at the palace!"

At the sound of her voice the dragon opened his eyes again, but now Bridget was a long way off; against the sky all the dragon could see was her grey dress and the grey lining of her hat, which he took for a cloud.

He flew off to hunt for the escaped cat, but he flew off in the wrong direction.

In no time at all Bridget was back at the palace, where the Queen was so glad to have her cat returned that she could think of nothing else but giving him his breakfast and washing the sand off his paws. She told Bridget to come back another day about the petticoat.

So Bridget wished herself home again, stepping out on her right foot.

Back at home, she found that Solomon had woken up, and was just finishing her bowl of porridge, having eaten his own already.

The first thing he said was,

"Where did you get those boots?"

"Aren't they lovely?" said Bridget. "The King of the Grasshoppers gave them to me. They are wishing boots; they take you wherever you want to go."

She slipped them off her feet, for even the best new boots make your feet a little tired when you have been wearing them for an hour or two, and besides, Bridget was used to going barefoot all the time.

As she took them off, she noticed that a couple of gold coins from the dragon's hoard were sticking to the sole of the right boot.

"*That's* a piece of luck," she said. "The Queen hasn't paid me for her petticoat yet, and I didn't like to remind her. I'll just run down to the corner shop with these and buy something for dinner."

She took the money and ran down the road barefoot, leaving her boots on the back step.

Directly she was out of sight, Solomon tried on the boots. They fitted him excellently, for, being Bridget's twin, he had feet exactly the same size.

"What a good thing we are twins," thought Solomon. "These boots go much better with my blue velvet trousers than my old antelope ones. And it's handy that they are wishing boots, too."

He said aloud, "I wish to go to the place where Bridget picked up those gold coins," stepping out at the same time on to his left foot.

All the grasshoppers stopped their chirping and watched him whizz away.

The boots took him directly to the dragon's nest, and set him down by the blue pool. Then they melted from his feet like black wax, and that was the end of them. The two diamonds rolled into the dragon's hoard, where they still are.

The dragon woke up—he had come home very tired and peevish after vainly hunting all over the desert for the Queen's cat—and he was not particularly pleased to find Solomon in his nest. But he put him to work: he made Solomon sing him to sleep; and every time Solomon stopped singing the dragon opened his large red eyes and snapped, "Go on! I wasn't asleep!"

Solomon soon became hoarse, and very tired of singing, but the boots were gone and there was no way to escape; he had to make the best of things.

Meanwhile, when Bridget got back from the grocer's and found both Solomon and the boots missing, she became very anxious. But she had not been worrying for long when a carriage pulled up at the door, and the white-wigged coachman gave her a note in the Queen's writing:

My Dear Bridget,
    as a reward for finding Puss, would you like to come and live here and be our Court Dress-maker? If so, please get into the carriage and come back at once.
                Georgina R

"Oh dear," thought Bridget, "but what about Solomon?"

At that moment the King of the Grasshoppers jumped on to her shoulder.

"Don't trouble yourself about Solomon, my dear Bridget," he told her.

"Oh, your Majesty! Is he all right? I'm afraid he may have gone off in the boots you gave me and I hadn't warned him about them."

"He is quite all right. He has found exactly the right job," said the King of the Grasshoppers. "And to tell you the truth, we are very pleased to be rid of him here, for he was eating all our grass blades and quite drowned our voices with his snoring. Now goodbye, my dear Bridget; enjoy yourself at the palace."

So Bridget put on her beautiful hat and rode off in the carriage. As she drove through the town the Mayor's son, looking out of his window, saw her and fell bang in love with her. Three weeks

later he proposed to her, she accepted, they were married, and lived happily ever after.

But even after she was married she went on making hats and petticoats and handkerchiefs for the Queen, and for her own friends, because she enjoyed making things and did it so well.

As for Solomon, he soon found out that the dragon could be put to sleep by the sound of snoring even more easily than by the sound of singing (if the truth be known the dragon preferred Solomon's snores to his songs) and so for the rest of their days they lay side by side, fast asleep, on the edge of the blue pool, under the great rose-tree with its pink blossoms.

The Goodbye Song

Once there was a mother who had three sons: a soldier, a sailor and a coal-miner. Every day the soldier went off to fight in some battle, and the sailor went fishing in the rough sea, and the miner went down into the deep dark dangerous tunnels of the mine to dig for coal.

At first the mother used to worry about her sons very much when they went off, and wonder if they'd ever come safely home. But one night, out of the depths of her worry, she dreamed a song, and the next day, when she woke up, she remembered the words of it, and the tune.

These were the words:

> Road, river, mountain, sea,
> Bring my boys safe to me
> Earth, air, sun, moon,
> Bring my sons back soon
> Luck, chance, wish, will
> Keep them safe from all ill.

Now these words, together with the tune that she also dreamed, which was a very sweet, strange air, combined to make a strong magic charm.

Every day, when the boys went off, their mother would sing her goodbye song, and it kept her sons safe from all harm. Even in the fiercest battle, no arrow or bullet ever touched the soldier. Even in the worst storm the sailor's boat never let in a drop of water, but swung over the waves and carried him back to harbour. And even in the most dangerous part of the mine, even when the rock roof gave way, even when underground water burst out of a hole in the wall, even when there was poisonous gas, or when he got lost in one of a hundred narrow passages all alike, the miner son remembered his mother's song, and never gave up hope. Somehow he managed to escape every danger, and always returned safe to the ground above.

After many years the mother grew very old and died, and her three sons also grew old and died, each safe in his own home.

But in the meantime they had married, and had wives and sons. And the wives, and the sons' wives, in their turn, learned the family song, and sang it when their children went away from home, to keep them safe from harm.

But the grandmother had given them a warning, when she grew near to dying.

"Use the song as often as you like, my dear children. But never tell the secret to anyone outside our family. Never sell it for money."

And the sons, and the sons' wives, promised

they would never do such a thing. And they never did. But their children, too, learned the song in time, and one of the children was a greedy boy, who always wanted more than he had, who never enjoyed what was happening today, because he hoped tomorrow would be better, and who could never bear to see anybody else given a present, even if it was something he didn't want himself.

His brothers and sisters and his cousins called him Soapy Sam because of a time when he was smaller and had tried to eat the soap in the bath, thinking that as it had a nice smell it must be good to eat.

One day Soapy Sam happened to be all alone in the house when a very smiling stranger came to the door.

"I have heard around the town that you have a family song, which will protect the person who hears it from all harm," said this smiling stranger.

"Sure," said Soapy Sam, not very interested, because he was wondering how soon his mother would get back from shopping and make the lunch. I hope it's fried potatoes, he thought.

"I'd like to make a recording of the song. I'll pay handsomely for it. My name's Pennyquick," said the smiling caller.

"It isn't allowed," said Soapy Sam. "Mum wouldn't allow it. Nor would Dad."

"I'd give a tremendous lot to hear it," said Mr Pennyquick. "I wish you'd sing it to me."

"What would you give?"

"What would you like?"

"Fried potatoes for every meal for the rest of my life."

"All right. If that's what you want most, that can easily be arranged," said Mr Pennyquick, getting out a little tape-recorder.

"Once we have this song recorded it'll make our fortunes. I promise you fried potatoes three times a day for the rest of your life."

"Promises are one thing," said Soapy Sam. "Real fried potatoes are another."

But at that very moment an old man came along the street pushing his tin trolley, which had a brazier burning under it, and was full of hot fried

potatoes. Everybody in the town called the old man Mr Thunder, because his trolley made such a noise, clanking along over the cobbles.

"Here you are," said Mr Pennyquick. "Here's the first instalment," and he bought twopence-worth of fried potatoes and handed them to Soapy Sam.

"Twopence-worth is all very well for now," said Sam, "but what about the rest of my life?" And he opened the hot greasy bag and stuffed fried potatoes into his mouth as fast as he could.

"It'd cost thirty thousand pound to feed *that* boy on fried potatoes for the rest of his life," said old Mr Thunder.

"Just at this moment I haven't any more money on me," said Mr Pennyquick. "But in a week or so when we've recorded the song and I've sold the rights, I'll be able to pay you—"

"Tell you what," said old Mr Thunder. "Find me a bed I can sleep sound on, and I'll supply the fried potatoes free. For no bed that I've ever tried suits me, and my old woman says I snore louder than the trolley."

"I'll see what I can do," said Mr Pennyquick. He went to the town's largest bed store.

"What is the best bed you have?" he asked the owner, a Mr Trestle.

"Our best model, this one, has a silver frame and Chinese silk sheets. The mattress is woven of triple-mesh spiderwebs and filled inside with

rose-leaf jelly," Mr Trestle said. "It is so comfortable that a man has been known to lie down and go
to sleep on it even when being chased by a lion.
And the lion lay right down and went to sleep
beside him."

"I'll have it. What does it cost?" said Mr
Pennyquick.

"Thirty thousand pounds," Mr Trestle told
him. "It sounds dear I know, but it's on account
of the labour. Collecting all the spiderwebs and
making the rose-leaf jelly is a slow job."

"I haven't any money just at this moment,"
said Mr Pennyquick, "but next week when I've
finished a deal on a top hit-song, I'll be able to let

62

you have thirty thousand."

"We won't worry about that," said Mr Trestle. "Tell you what, you find me a book that I can read every evening without getting bored, and you can have the bed for love. I'm so tired of my own thoughts in the evenings that I'd send away my head for a football if any team would take it."

"I'll see what I can do," said Mr Pennyquick, and he went to a bookshop.

"I'm looking for something that a person could read every evening without getting bored," he said.

The bookseller, a young fellow called Fred Page, was writing so hard in a big black notebook that even after Mr Pennyquick spoke, it took him a minute to lift his head.

"Book? Book?" he said then. "You can have this one I'm writing. It's just finished. It's the best

book in the world, no question. I'm expecting to make fifty thousand on the film rights alone. But you can have it for thirty."

"Well I haven't any money on me at the moment—" said Mr Pennyquick, "but—"

A very pretty girl walked past them out of the shop with a basket on her arm.

"I'll tell you," said Fred Page, "you give me a charm to keep my wife safe while she's shopping, and you can have the book free. For I worry about her all the time when she's out of my sight."

"I'll be able to give you exactly what you want tomorrow," said Mr Pennyquick.

"Done!" said the bookseller, and he passed over the notebook filled with black scrawled handwriting. Mr Pennyquick carried it to the bed-store, where Mr Trestle received it with some surprise, and arranged to have his best bed delivered right away to Mr Thunder. When the old fried-potato seller received the bed, he wrote on a bit of greaseproof paper:

In return for a guaranteed night's sound sleep I hereby agree to supply fried potatoes to Soapy Sam three times a day for the rest of his life

Mr Pennyquick took the bit of paper to Soapy Sam.

"I can't read," said Soapy Sam, so Mr Pennyquick read the words to him.

"Now," he said, "take this tape-recorder and sing the goodbye song."

"I can't sing," said Soapy Sam. "Don't know one note from another. Can't remember the tune."

Mr Pennyquick was rather annoyed at that, but he said,

"Well, then you must hide the tape-recorder in the coat rack, so as to get a recording of your mother singing it in the morning when you all go off to school."

However, Soapy Sam hid the tape-recorder in his school bag. Next morning he quickly and secretly switched it on just before his mother sang her goodbye:

"Road, river, mountain, sea,
Bring my kids back safe to me
Earth, air, sun, moon,
Bring my children back soon
Luck, chance, wish, will
Keep them safe from all ill."

Then, as soon as he was out of sight of the house, Soapy Sam switched off the tape-recorder, ran to a street-corner where Mr Pennyquick had arranged to meet him, handed over the recorder, and ran on.

At the next corner he came across old Mr Thunder, who was pushing his trolley along, looking very thoughtful. Sam asked for his next serving of fried potatoes, and got them, in a twist of greasy paper.

But now a queer thing happened to Soapy Sam. As he walked the rest of the way to school, eating the fried potatoes in his fingers, he suddenly discovered that he didn't like fried potatoes any longer. In fact they made him feel sick, and he had to throw half of them away; he couldn't eat them.

And when he came home from school and his mother said:

"There's fried potatoes for dinner, your favourite," Sam turned quite pale, and said,

"I feel terrible. I don't want any dinner. I'm going upstairs to bed."

The thought of having fried potatoes three times a day for the rest of his life was more than he could bear. And indeed, he never touched them again.

Meanwhile old Mr Thunder had found Mr Pennyquick, and said,

"I'm sorry, but that bed's no use to me. I did sleep, but I had terrible nightmares the whole night through: shipwrecks, and landslides, and plagues, and people killing each other in battles. I'm afraid you'll have to find me another bed."

"Oh indeed?" said Mr Pennyquick, rather

annoyed. "Well, you'll have to be patient just a little while."

Then Mr Trestle the bedmaker came along and said to Mr Pennyquick,

"I've been looking for you. That book you gave me won't do. I can't even read the writing. You'll have to find me another."

"Oh, very well," snapped Mr Pennyquick. "Just be patient a little longer, will you?"

Then Fred Page the bookseller came along and said,

"Hey! What about that song you promised me in exchange for my book?"

"You can have your book back," said Mr Pennyquick.

"I don't want it back. I've begun writing another. I want the song."

"All right, I'll play it here and now," said Mr Pennyquick, and he switched on the tape-recorder.

But no song came out of it—only a broken, jangled noise, like forks being rattled together inside an iron basin.

"*That's* no good to me," said Fred Page.

"It's no good to me either," said Mr Penny-quick angrily, and he hurried off in search of Soapy Sam. But Sam's mother answered the door this time, and she said,

"Sam is sick in bed with measles. He can't see anybody. Who are you, anyway? Are you from the school?"

One look at Sam's mother told Mr Pennyquick that he'd never get the song from *her*.

There was nothing for it but to leave town and try his luck somewhere else, and that he did.

Mr Thunder gave the silver bed back to Mr Trestle, who gave the book back to Fred Page, who went on worrying about his wife till the end of his days.

And next morning when Sam's mother started to sing the song to her other children as they left for school, she found that she could recall neither the tune nor the words, and no more could anybody else in the family; nor did it ever come back to them.

The goodbye song was gone for good.

The Queen of the Moon

Once there was a girl called Tansy whose father was a digger. Whenever people wanted a road dug up, to lay pipes, or a space cleared, to build a house, Tansy's father, and other men as well, would do the digging. Tansy hadn't any mother, so while the men dug she found things to do on the edge of the earthy, dusty place where they were at work.

She built castles out of the stones they dug up, or made patterns out of the bits of glass and china. Sometimes she found old arrowheads, or old broken clay pipes, or old bones. Once or twice she found an old coin, but her father always took those, saying he would show them to a museum, and perhaps get money for them. Tansy never heard if he did.

Tansy and her father never had much money, because diggers don't get paid much. They lived in a box on wheels that was meant for moving horses. Tansy's father had found it at a crossroads, and, as it was not too heavy to pull, he dragged it away. It made a useful home; there was room in it for two bunks, though not much else. When the weather was wet, Tansy and her father had breakfast, mostly bread-and-jam, lying in their bunks. When it was fine they ate outside. And they pulled the horse-box to wherever Tansy's father happened to be doing his digging.

Just now he was digging in London, on a huge wide space that would one day be covered with a grand new vegetable market. It was so big that there would be work for months ahead, so he was pleased about the job. Tansy was not so happy. She did not care for this great open windy, dusty place in the middle of the city.

"Shame about it, really," her father said once. "Used to be all streets, here, long ago, people's houses, lots of them. Your great-great-grandma lived round here, years back."

"Did she?" said Tansy. "What was her name?"

"Dido, like your ma. But she married some rich bloke and moved away."

After that, Tansy hunted in the dust even more carefully, in hopes she might find something that had once belonged to her great-great-grandma. And she did find a little lead spoon that, if you looked very hard and believed very hard, had something scratched on it that might be the letters D-I-D-O.

"What does Dido mean?" she asked her father.

"Dunno," he said, filling his pipe with tobacco. "Maybe it means died, like your ma."

But one of Tansy's father's mates, a boy called Morgan who was digging to earn money for college, said that Dido was a queen's name.

Maybe the rich bloke that great-great-grandma married was a king, Tansy thought.

"What does Tansy mean?" she asked Morgan.

A lady they had lodged with once, before they got the horse-box, had said that Tansy was a very odd name, and not at all common.

"It's a flower, a kind of flower that grows on waste places. It looks something like a daisy."

"What does a daisy look like?"

"Haven't you ever seen a *daisy*?"

"Dunno," said Tansy. "There aren't any round here, are there?"

"No," said Morgan, looking round the huge dusty place where they stood. "That's true. Well, if your dad doesn't mind, I'll take you to see some on Sunday."

Tansy's dad didn't mind at all. He liked to spend his Sundays sleeping. So on Sunday Tansy and Morgan caught a bus into the country, where Tansy had never been, for digging jobs are mostly in towns, and Tansy's dad always chose the town ones if he had a choice.

They got out of the bus and walked along a road, past a little church, and across a farmyard where hens were pecking about and doves sat on a wall, making a contented peaceful noise as if they were clearing their throats. Green feathery plants grew at the side of the yard. They had white-and-yellow flowers which gave off a strong musky sweetish smell in the warm sun.

"That's tansy," said Morgan, "that white-and-yellow stuff. And now—look—here's daisies."

They had come to the edge of a field, where grass grew as high as Tansy's chest. Among the grass, and so thick that the field was white with them, were single flowers the size of eyes, or egg-yolks—hundreds and thousands and millions and billions and trillions of them. They had a calm smell—not so sweet as the tansy, but comfortable, like toast. Up above the sun shone, and somewhere a bird hung in the sky and sang the same song over and over.

"Are these daisies?" Tansy looked at the flowers, which were almost up to her chin.

"Those are moon daisies."

"I suppose they grow like that on the moon too."

"Maybe."

Tansy and Morgan ate the sausage rolls he had brought, and then he lay down in a clump of grass at the edge of the field and went to sleep. Tansy walked along the side of the field till she came to a little stream. She built a dam out of sticks and mud. Then she built an island out of stones, and put smaller stones and earth on top. Over the earth she laid green moss, and then she picked moon daisies and stuck them into the moss. They looked as if they were growing. She had to wade up to her knees, and her jeans got rather wet. She took off her vest to carry loads of stones and earth in it.

The stones made more holes in the vest, but there had been holes in it anyway.

Then Morgan woke up and told her to put her vest back on, and they caught the bus back to London.

That night Tansy slept badly and she had a queer dream.

She dreamed that she was on the moon, which was as big and round as a circus ring, and flat and shining, and covered all over with white flowers.

In the middle, picking flowers, was a girl about Tansy's size.

"Hullo," said this girl. "I'm Dido. What's your name?"

"Tansy," said Tansy.

"Oh, then you must be my great-great-granddaughter."

"I've got your spoon," said Tansy, and took it out of her jeans pocket.

"So you have," said Dido, looking at it carefully. "I used to eat my porridge with that, when I lived in Nine Elms. Now I'm Queen of the Moon."

"Do you like that?"

"It's not bad. I can pick all the flowers I want, and eat moon-candy and ice-cream moondaes, and listen to the moon birds, and ride moon-horses."

"It's nice here," said Tansy.

"Well you can come whenever you like, so long as you have my spoon."

"Thank you, great-great-grandma," said Tansy, putting the spoon back in her pocket.

"That's all right," Dido said. "You can call me Dido, if you like."

Next day when Tansy woke she remembered this dream. After that, she always made sure that she had the little lead spoon safe in her pocket.

That day, and for some days after, she felt stiff and tired, and achey in her arms and legs, so she didn't go out to the dusty site where the men were digging, but lay in her bunk and thought about the moon all covered in white daisies.

Every night that week she dreamed about the

77

moon. Dido was there, and they picked the white flowers, and rode the white horses, and drank moon-milk, and talked all night long.

Next week Tansy felt even stiffer, and her throat was sore. She stayed in her bunk again, all the time her father was digging. And by the end of that week she felt so ill that she wasn't sure of anything except that she hurt all over, and once when she opened her eyes she wasn't in the horse-box at all but in a white room with a lot of white people.

"Am I in the moon?" said Tansy.

"No, not in the moon. Go back to sleep, dear," someone said. "You'll soon be better."

Tansy shut her eyes again, and went back to the moon, where Dido was waiting for her. She stayed for quite a long visit this time.

When she opened her eyes next, a voice said,

"Now you're feeling better, aren't you?"

"Yes, thank you," said Tansy, for the soreness in her throat and the ache in her arms and legs had gone. She still felt weak, but she was able to sit up in bed and eat boiled egg and bread-and-butter and apple sauce.

"You're in hospital, did you know?" said the nurse giving Tansy her boiled egg. "I bet you were surprised to find yourself here. You've been quite ill with fever."

"The first time I woke," Tansy said, "I thought I was in the moon. But this isn't a bit like the moon

really."

"I should think not," said the nurse. "The moon's all dry and dusty."

"No it isn't!" said Tansy. "The moon's all covered with daisies."

"No daisies on the moon, love," said the nurse. "No flowers at all."

"How do *you* know," said Tansy disbelievingly.

"Why, there's been people up there," said the nurse. "Walking about and taking pictures. Haven't you seen them? I think there are some in one of the books at the end of the ward."

She went and hunted in a pile of books and magazines and brought one back.

"Here, see? These men are on the moon. That's their space-ship."

Tansy looked at the pictures of the dusty place. Then she said she felt tired and wanted to lie down. Just then her father came in to visit her. He said he was going to get a job in the country where they could live on a farm and eat real hens' eggs. But Tansy was too tired to talk much.

Later, when it was dark and she was being settled for the night, Tansy asked the nurse,

"Where's my little spoon?"

"That dirty little lead one? Your father took it away with some other stuff you don't need here. He'll have it for you safe at home," the nurse said.

But Tansy wasn't so sure. Her father was careless, sometimes.

That night she found it hard to get to sleep, and when she did sleep she dreamed about such an empty, dusty place that she woke up fast, quite out of breath, as if the dust were choking her.

The nurse had gone, so Tansy climbed out of bed and began hunting for the little spoon, just in case her father had dropped it. But she could not see it. She was thirsty, so, looking for the nurse, she went out of the room and along a wide passage with dim lights. Nobody was in sight. Tansy went on and on, and she was crying a little, because she was so thirsty, and she so badly needed to find her spoon. Even if she did find it, would she be able to get back to the place where she had met Dido? For if the pictures that the nurse had shown her were of the real moon, then where was Dido's moon?

Not looking where she was going, Tansy ran slap into a man wearing a white coat.

"Hey!" he said. "Where are you off to?"

"I'm looking for the moon," Tansy said.

"I wouldn't go there, not if I was you," said the man. "It's a nasty place. All dry and cold. Or so I understand."

At that, Tansy fairly burst out crying. "Not *my* moon!" she said. "*My* moon's a *nice* place, all covered in white flowers, and there's streams and islands, and you can drink moondew and eat moonberries."

"Can you though?" said the white-coated man.

"Oddly enough that sounds just like a place that *I've* just been studying. Want to see? I dare say people are hunting for you high and low, but a couple more minutes won't make all that difference. Come in here a moment."

He led Tansy into a big room with lots of tables and lots of jars and tubes on them. On one table was a tall black question-mark-shaped thing with an eye-piece.

"Climb on this chair," said the man, "put your eye *there*, shut the other eye, slowly turn the screw, and tell me what you see."

Tansy climbed on the chair, shut one eye, put the other one to the eye-piece, and turned the screw. First what she saw was just colours, all misty at the edge like the rainbow, and then, quite suddenly, there was a field of daisies, and a river, and a hill and a silver tree.

"Why!" she said. "It is! It's my moon—or somewhere just like it!"

"See? What did I tell you? Where did you find *your* moon?" said the man.

"I dreamed it. But the nurse said the real moon doesn't have daisies."

"Now look," said the man. "If you dreamed it, it must be real. Right? There isn't only *one* moon, you know. Why, space is stuffed with moons, all sizes, and then there are a lot of really small ones as well. This one you're looking at is in a drop of milk. Milk's full of moons. So are you! So don't

you worry—you're sure to find your special moon
somewhere. Now I'd better take you back to
bed."

Back in the ward, the nurses were hunting for
her, high and low.

"My goodness, where have you been?" they
said. "We were worried to death."

"She popped along to me to check up on something," said the white-coated man. "She'd lost
the moon and she wanted me to put it back. Now
you go to sleep," he said to Tansy. "Stop worrying,
and in the morning I'll bring you along a few
more moons to look at, and a glass to look at them
through."

"What was he going on about?" said Tansy's
nurse, when he had gone. "He's a weird one, that

Mr Smith from pathology. Lost the moon, what nonsense, when there it is, large as a soup-plate, right outside the window! Now, you have a drink and get back into bed at once. Here's your little spoon—your father left it at the porter's desk after all. Said he thought you liked to have it by you for a lucky charm. Off to sleep now, and don't let's have any more trouble from *you* tonight."

Tansy got back into bed, holding her little spoon tight, and when the nurse had gone she lay looking at the great silvery plateful of moon that hung in the sky just outside her window.

"Even if that isn't *my* moon," she thought as her eyes closed, "it's a nice colour. And I expect that Mr Smith's right ... I'm sure to find my own moon somewhere, with Dido on it ..."

Clean Sheets

Once there was a boy called Gus, and his mother said to him,

"Gus, it's the day for clean sheets. Take the blankets off your bed, hang them out of the window in the sun, take off the sheets and pillowcases, and turn the mattress. Don't forget to fold the sheets and pillowcases, ready to send to the laundry, but first give them a good shake."

"Why, Ma?" said Gus.

"In case any living creature, a bee or a spider or a fly, has got in among them. We wouldn't want to send a living creature to the laundry."

"That's true," said Gus, hoping very much that he *wouldn't* find a bee or a spider or a cockroach in his bedclothes.

He hung the blankets out of the window to air. Then he took off the top sheet and folded it, ends together, sides together, held the fold under his chin, and folded it again into a neat square.

When he took off the bottom sheet and shook it, out fell no living creature but a prickly leaf, blue as a forget-me-not.

"That's a funny-looking leaf," said Gus, and he showed it to his mother.

"What a queer leaf," she said. "I've never seen one like it before. Where can it have come from?"

"Must have blown in the window. I'll show it to my teacher at school," said Gus. "Maybe he will know."

The teacher at school didn't know what kind of a leaf it was either, but he said, "Why not take it to old Mr Brown at the antiquarian bookshop. He's read so many books, he might know. Besides, he has a collection of rare plants."

So Gus took the prickly blue leaf to old Mr Brown, who looked at it through his glasses, and through a lens. Then he said,

"My boy, you've got a treasure there. What you

have is a leaf from the Memory Tree."

"What's the Memory Tree?"

"It grows in the forests of Brazil. Have you had any Brazil nuts lately?"

"We did have some," said Gus.

"A leaf might have got among them. The tree was found once, but then it was lost again. Nobody knows where it grows. Just sometimes, once in a way, a leaf turns up."

"What does it do?"

"If you hold it scrunched up in your hand, you can remember anything."

"Anything in the world?"

"Anything in the world."

"Even if it hasn't happened?"

"Even if it hasn't happened."

Gus quickly scrunched up the Memory leaf in his hand. The prickles hurt a little, but not too badly.

"Now, say what you want to remember," said Mr Brown.

"I want to remember how I was given a zebra for my birthday," said Gus, "and how I rode it right through the town, crossing all the traffic lights when they were red ..."

Right away, that very minute, he could remember his birthday, and how he had looked out of his window to see the zebra standing tied to the front door-knocker. He could remember the zebra's name, Horace, and his red saddle and

bridle, with brass bits, and the way all the motorists had hooted when Horace galloped across the lights, and how the police had started after him on their motorbikes but he had been much too fast for them to catch up.

"My goodness," Gus said to Mr Brown. "I didn't think memories could be as exciting as that. Now you have a try."

He unclenched his hand. Instantly the Memory leaf unscrumpled and went back to its proper shape. Mr Brown took it and scrunched it up in *his* hand.

"I want to remember every minute of my first visit to Venice," he said.

"Why don't you remember something that *didn't* happen?" said Gus.

"When you get to my age," said Mr Brown, "you have plenty of things that you are glad to remember without going to the trouble of inventing."

By the distant smile on his face, it was plain that he was having a very happy time remembering his first visit to Venice.

"Take good care of that leaf, my boy," he said. "You've got a treasure there and you're never likely to find another."

Gus took the leaf home and told his father and mother what it was.

"Fancy!" said his mother. "Just let me have it a moment so I can remember where I hid the key to my desk that time when we went to visit Aunt Alice five years ago."

She scrumpled up the leaf in her hand. Instantly she remembered that she had buried the key in a pot of geraniums. Unluckily the geraniums had died long ago and the pot of earth had been thrown away. But Gus's mother also remembered Cousin Flora's address in Minnesota, and the title of a book she had read about in a magazine and wanted to get from the library, and a recipe for chutney Mrs Swale had given her that she had forgotten to write down, and several things she had meant to tell the doctor about her rheumatism when she saw him the day before.

"Here, let me have a go," said Gus's father. And he scrunched up the leaf in his hand and remembered the name of the boy who had sat next to him in his first year at school, and a very good football match between Arsenal and Tottenham in 1948, and the taste of the date shortbreads that his grandmother used to make.

"Now it's my turn!" said Gus. "After all, I found the leaf."

"It's your bedtime," said his mother. So Gus had to go to bed, but he took the leaf with him. And lying in bed, holding the leaf scrunched up in his hand, he remembered floating down the Colorado river in a canoe past great golden cliffs. He remembered flying across the Gobi desert on the back of an eagle. He remembered winning the Derby on the Queen's horse. He remembered getting ten out of ten for sums every day for a whole term. He remembered the sarcastic thing he had said to Mr Formby the history teacher. He remembered finding a sword stuck in a rock and pulling it out. He remembered scoring the winning goal in an ice-hockey match. He remembered getting into the pilot's seat of a small aeroplane he had been given. Then he went to sleep . . .

Next day he found the Memory leaf where it had slipped down to the bottom of the bed, and took it to school. He showed it to his best friend, Andrew, who had a go at using it, and remembered that a boy called Ted Stone owed him two packets of chewing-gum.

"That's a boring sort of thing to remember," said Gus.

Ted, when reminded about the gum, had a go at the leaf, and remembered eating all the dough-nuts in the world without being sick.

"Tell you what," said Andrew, "why don't you take it to the Queen?"

"Why?" said Gus. "What's the point? I'd rather keep it myself."

"Don't be stupid. Take it to the Queen, get her to hold it, and remind her how you found her crown when it was lost. Then you'll get the reward."

The Queen of that country was always losing her crown; generally it turned up quite soon, hanging on a lamp-post, or among the cabbages in a supermarket, or on a seat in the park or a hat-stand in a café, wherever she had happened to take it off.

Sometimes it didn't turn up, and then she had a new one made.

"But I never have found her crown," said Gus.

"No, but she'll remember if you tell her so."

Gus wasn't interested in the reward, but he was

quite pleased at a chance to see the Queen. So he brushed his hair and put on a clean jersey and went along to the palace on Saturday morning, at which time the Queen was always at home to any of her subjects who wanted to drop in and consult her.

"Good morning, your Majesty," said Gus, when he had passed all the guards and done the best bow he could.

"Good morning, what can I do for you?" said the Queen.

"I've brought this rare leaf for you to look at," said Gus. "Hold it scrunched up in your hand, your Majesty, and you'll be able to remember how I found your crown last time you lost it."

The Queen scrunched up the Memory leaf in her hand.

Then she frowned at Gus.

"Yes!" she said. "I can remember that you found my crown. I can also remember that you stuck it on your head and galloped right through the town on a zebra, passing all the traffic lights at red and causing unheard-of traffic chaos. What is more, when you *did* bring the crown back, it was badly dented, and several of the diamonds had fallen out."

"I-I'm sorry, Ma'am," stammered Gus, very much taken aback. "I d-don't remember that myself."

"In fact the fines that you owe for dangerous zebramanship exactly equal the amount that the reward would have been," said the Queen severely, giving him back the leaf, "and you are lucky I don't send you to prison for damaging royal property."

What she said made Gus so nervous that he dropped the leaf on to the marble floor.

A draught blew it clean out of the palace window, across the main square of the town, over the river, and far away, who knows where.

Gus never found a Memory leaf again.

Perhaps it was just as well.

The Alarm Cock

Once there was a shop with a sign over the door that said, VINE, WOLF, AND PARROTT, HELPERS.

If you opened the door and went in, you saw the Vine right away, for it grew out of the floor and up the walls of the little shop, so the whole room was lined with leaves, and clusters of flowers hung from the ceiling. Beautiful orange trumpet-shaped flowers they were, and the vine was covered with them all the year round.

The next thing you saw was Wolf. He was a real wolf, big and grey, with a handsome ruff round his neck, and he sat on the counter looking thoughtful and wise, with his long chin sunk on his shaggy grey chest.

And the last thing you saw was old Mr Parrott, who was not a bird but a grey-haired old man, generally at work in some corner of the shop, pruning the vine, or twining a new shoot so that it would grow comfortably up the wall.

Another sign, over the counter, said,

NO FEE UNLESS SATISFIED.

PAYMENT IN KIND ACCEPTED.

WE HELP YOU WITH ALL YOUR PROBLEMS.

And it was true, there were not many problems

that the firm of Vine, Wolf, and Parrott could not solve.

For instance one day a man came in to complain, "My dog sits up on the roof all day. Even at night he won't come down. What's the use of a dog who's never in the house and won't even come for a walk? Is something wrong with him?"

"Does he bark or howl?" asked Wolf.

"No, just sits watching the clouds and the birds."

"Wolf had better go and talk to him," said old Mr Parrott. "What is your address?"

"Eighty-four Smith Street."

So old Mr Parrott got out his bicycle, and a ladder, and bicycled along to Number Eighty-four Smith Street, with the ladder on his shoulder and Wolf sitting on one end of it, and he held the foot of the ladder while Wolf climbed up on to the roof to talk to the dog, and soon found out that he was annoyed because his master never watched greyhound racing on television, and so he had gone on a roof-strike, but would agree to come down if he might sometimes be allowed to watch his favourite TV programme.

A man came in to say, "My car has caught a cold. It keeps sneezing. What should I do?"

"Get it a warmer bonnet. And put socks on its tyres. And give it a basinful of this Car Cough Mixture night and morning."

A girl came in to say, "My record player has slowed down. Instead of the record going round

thirty-three times and a half every minute, it goes round once every thirty-three and a half minutes. What can I do about it?"

"You can slow down too," said old Mr Parrott, after consulting his partners. "Swallow this slow-down pill and then you'll be able to hear the music just as well as before."

The girl swallowed the pill, and it slowed her down so much that it took her half an hour to walk to the door of the shop, and she hasn't reached home yet.

An old lady who lived just along the street, Mrs Heyhoe, came in with her little grand-daughter. Mrs Heyhoe was called Anna, so was her grand-daughter, and there were exactly seventy years between them. One was seven, the other seventy-seven. And they both looked the same; fair hair, bright blue eyes, straight noses, rather short, very cheerful.

"What can I do for you, Mrs Heyhoe, ma'am?" said old Mr Parrott, while little Anna patted Wolf, who wagged his tail.

"I can't get to sleep, Mr Parrott. I haven't slept a wink these three weeks."

"Dear me," said Mr Parrott. "That's serious, that is. What you need is a nutmeg-scented fan. Buy a fan, soak it in nutmeg essence, fan yourself a hundred times, and that should do the trick."

"Shall I pay you now?" said old Mrs Heyhoe.

"No, no," he said, pointing to the sign, "not

until you are satisfied."

So old Mrs Heyhoe went down the road to a fan shop, where she and little Anna chose a very pretty fan, lace, painted all over with roses.

They ground up a hundred nutmegs in the mincer and made a strong nutmeg tea. They sprinkled the fan with nutmeg tea three times an hour for three days, and then at bedtime old Mrs Heyhoe fanned herself a hundred times. Then little Anna fanned her a hundred times. Then she fanned herself again. Little Anna went to sleep, but her grandmother stayed wide awake all night until the sun came in the kitchen window and turned all the teacloths pink.

She thought of all sorts of useful things during the night: where she had put her glasses, a way to use up all her old stockings by stuffing cushions with them, and five new ideas for puddings, but she went back to Mr Parrott, and said,

"The nutmeg fan didn't work."

"Dear me," he said. "It's not often that one of our suggestions doesn't work. Then you had better try playing the flute for half an hour, last thing before you go to bed, with your feet in a big bowl of honey."

Mrs Heyhoe tried that. She already had a flute that her son, Anna's father, had played when he was a boy. And she kept bees, so she had plenty of honey.

But her next-door neighbour came to the back

door, knocking, just when Mrs Heyhoe had got her feet into the honey, to say that Anna's father had called up on her telephone, and was wishful to speak to his mum, who hadn't got a phone.

So that was a nuisance, and it took Mrs Heyhoe quite a long time to get the honey from between her toes, and even so some got spilt on the kitchen floor, and after all, her son only wanted to know if little Anna was behaving herself.

"Which I am, aren't I, Granny?" said little Anna.

"Beautifully, my dearie."

Then they found that the flute had fallen into the honey.

And that night again Mrs Heyhoe didn't sleep a wink.

"Really," said old Mr Parrott, when she went back to him next day. "I don't know that we've ever had a more awkward case. You had better try sniffing at a clove orange, while at the same time imagining that you are inside a teapot."

So Mrs Heyhoe and Anna bought a whole lot of cloves and made two clove oranges (one for little Anna to take to her mother when she went home). They stuck the cloves all over the oranges, so tight together that you couldn't get a pin between them.

Mrs Heyhoe's kitchen smelt delicious, with the oranges, and the cloves, and the honey, and the nutmeg fan, which they had put up over the fireplace.

At bedtime Mrs Heyhoe shut her eyes and sniffed one of the oranges, and imagined that she was inside a teapot.

But next morning she went back to Vine, Wolf, and Parrott.

"It didn't work," she told Mr Parrott. "That was the dirtiest teapot I've ever been inside. I had to spend the whole night scrubbing to get it clean. Never had a wink of sleep the whole night long."

"Humph," said old Mr Parrott. "This certainly is a serious case."

He consulted again with his partners.

"If we could find out *why* Mrs Heyhoe can't get to sleep," said the Vine in her soft voice, "we might be able to suggest the cure for her trouble."

When the Vine spoke, her voice came out through all of her trumpet-shaped orange flowers.

"*Why* can't you get to sleep, ma'am?" asked old Mr Parrott.

"Because I'm so worried about waking up in time," said old Mrs Heyhoe.

"Then," said the Vine, "what she needs is an alarm cock."

"What's that?" said little Anna.

"A rooster alarm clock. You've heard of a cuckoo clock? A rooster clock is just the same. Only, instead of going Cuckoo, it goes Cock-a-doodle-doo, and wakes you up."

"Well," said old Mrs Heyhoe, "we had better get one."

So she and little Anna walked all over the town, going to each clock shop in turn. But nowhere could they find a rooster alarm clock. They could find owl clocks and pigeon clocks, nightingale clocks and ostrich clocks, peacock clocks, lark, duck, and chick clocks, moorcock, blackcock and woodcock clocks, but not a single shop had a plain cock clock.

"I wonder," said little Anna presently, "if just an ordinary rooster wouldn't do as well, like the one Daddy has at home?"

"But where should we find a rooster in the town?" said her granny.

"Well," said little Anna, "as we walk along, I'm sure I can sometimes hear a rooster going Cock-a-doodle-doo."

"It would be a funny thing if you could," said her granny, "right in the middle of the town." But she began to listen, she listened and she listened, and by and by she thought she could hear a rooster somewhere going Cock-a-doodle-doo.

"It seems to be loudest in this street," said little Anna.

They were in Smith Street.

They walked north, and the crowing got fainter. So then they walked west, along Jones Street, and it grew louder. Then it grew fainter, so they walked south along Brown Street, till it grew louder. Then it grew fainter, so they walked east along Robinson Street.

"Now we're back where we began, in Smith Street," said little Anna.

"It's a puzzle," said old Mrs Heyhoe.

"*I* believe the rooster's up above," said little Anna.

They looked up. They had been walking round a big building which took up a whole city block. The building was fifty storeys high—so high that,

as it was a misty
day, the top was out
of sight in the
clouds.

"*I* think we'll have to
go up," said little
Anna.

So they walked
through the main
entrance of the
building, and went up.
They went up in
a lift, and at each
floor they stepped
out and asked the
people there,

"Do you know of a
rooster living on this
floor?"

Nobody knew of
a rooster—not on the
fifth floor, nor the
tenth, nor the
twentieth, nor the
twenty-fifth, nor
the thirtieth, nor
the fortieth.

At last they reached
the fiftieth floor and
stepped

out through a little door on to the roof, right above the clouds.

And there on the roof was a tiny cottage, with an old man sitting in the doorway peeling potatoes, and beside the door in the sunshine, sitting on an upside-down basket, was a beautiful glossy red rooster, with black and green feathers in his wings, and a black, blue, and green tail, and black legs, and a red cockscomb.

Little Anna ran to the cottage door.

"Oh, please," she said to the old man, busy peeling his potatoes, "could we buy your rooster?"

"Cock-a-doodle-doo!" shouted the rooster indignantly. "Nobody's going to buy me!"

"No indeed!" said the old man. "How would I be able to wake in the mornings without my rooster?"

"Besides," said the rooster, "I'm happy up here above the clouds. I wouldn't *dream* of living down below where it's all misty and grey. Up here the sun shines all day and the moon shines all night."

Little Anna and her granny looked at each other sadly.

"They are right, you know," said old Mrs Heyhoe. "Why should the old man lose his rooster? And why should the rooster live below the clouds if he doesn't want to?"

But little Anna thought again and said to the old man, "I suppose we couldn't *rent* your rooster, just for a week or two, till my granny gets into the habit of sleeping again?"

And she said to the rooster, "The sun does shine down there sometimes. And Granny makes very good mashed potato."

"Why, if you put it like that," said the old man, whose name was Mr Welladay, "that doesn't sound such a bad idea. In fact it sounds like a very *good* idea. I've been feeling rather tired lately; I could do with a few weeks' sleep."

"Well," said the rooster, whose name was Enrico, "since you put it that way, that doesn't sound like a bad idea at all. In fact it would be very pleasant to get down out of the hot sun for a week or two."

"What sort of rent would you like?" asked old Mrs Heyhoe.

"How about a nice chocolate cake?" asked old Mr Welladay.

So they went home, back down the lift, back along the street, with Enrico sitting on little Anna's shoulder. And Mrs Heyhoe at once baked a nice big chocolate cake, and little Anna took it back to Mr Welladay, who just had time to eat it before he fell fast asleep.

That evening, after they had all had supper— Enrico had cornflakes and milk, so did little Anna —old Mrs Heyhoe, too, fell fast asleep in her armchair, and slept there the whole night through, very peacefully, until Enrico woke her at seven next morning, shouting,

"Cock-a-doodle-doo! It's time to wake up and make my breakfast."

Every night for seven nights old Mrs Heyhoe slept soundly. And every morning for seven mornings, Enrico woke her in the same way. On the eighth morning, he woke her by shouting,

"Cock-a-doodle-doo! It's time to get up and put little Anna on the train to go home!"

"Oh, thank goodness you woke me," said old Mrs Heyhoe. "I've been worrying about getting Anna on to that train this month past."

"Is *that* why you couldn't sleep while I've been staying with you, Granny?" said little Anna.

"Of course it is!" said old Mrs Heyhoe.

So they walked to the station, and little Anna got on to the train, with her bag of clothes, and a sandwich, and an apple, and the clove orange for her mother, and she blew a kiss and waved and called out, "Goodbye, Granny! Thank you for the lovely visit!"

Then old Mrs Heyhoe. went along to Vine, Wolf, and Parrott, to thank them for their help. She had made another chocolate cake to pay them, as Mr Welladay had enjoyed his so much. Mr Parrott shared it with Wolf, as the Vine did not eat cake.

And then Mrs Heyhoe took Enrico back to old Mr Welladay, who had enjoyed his long sleep so much that he said,

"You are welcome to borrow my rooster again

whenever your grand-daughter comes to visit. If Enrico agrees, of course."

"Certainly I agree," said Enrico. "Mrs Heyhoe makes the best mashed potato I ever tasted. And little Anna polished my comb every night. Whenever her grand-daughter is here on a visit, I'll be glad to oblige Mrs Heyhoe."

"And I'll be glad to have you," said Mrs Heyhoe.

So that is what they did.

The Tractor,
the Duck and the Drum

Once there was a boy called Euan, and it was going to be his birthday next week. He wanted a tractor that he could sit on, and it would go chug-chugging along. He wanted a drum that he could play on, rub-a-dub, rub-a-dub. And he wanted a real live duck that would swim in his bath and go quack, quack.

So he sat down and wrote a letter to his Aunt Bertha. His Aunt Bertha kept a wishing-spoon in her kitchen drawer. Wishing-spoons have a little shape like a shield at the back, where the spoon part joins on to the handle,
so they look like this:

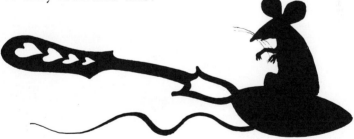

If you stir a cake, before it is cooked, with a wishing-spoon, there is a good chance that your wish will come true.

So Euan wrote to his Aunt Bertha:

DERE ANT BIRTHDAY
I SHD BEE VERRY GREAT
FULL IF U CD SEND MEE
A TRACK TOR

I CAN RIDE ON WAT GOES
CHUG CHUG CHUG & A
DRUM

I CAN PLAY ON
WAT GOES RUB A DUB DUB
& A DUK

TO SWIM IN MY BARF
WAT GOES QUAK QUAK QUAK
HOPE YOR ROOM A TIZ IZ BETR
LUV FRUM EUAN

and he folded the letter neatly in four, and put it in an envelope, and put a stamp on it, and posted it off to his Aunt Bertha.

His Aunt Bertha was a very absent-minded lady, and she was hasty, too. When the letter came she put down her knitting and she took her scissors and she slit the envelope open, and by doing that she cut Euan's letter into four bits.

"Here's a letter from my birthday nephew," said Aunt Bertha. "Let's see what he wants."

She took the four bits of paper and put them in a row, and read them.

"Now here's a puzzle," said Aunt Bertha. "For he seems to want a duck he can ride on that will go rub-a-dub-dub. And he wants a tractor he can play on that will go quack-quack-quack. And he seems to want a drum that will swim in his bath and go chug-chug-chug. Who ever heard of a drum going chug-chug-chug? And I am sure it would not be at all good for a drum to put it in the bath."

Then she moved the four bits of paper into a different row, and read them again.

"But perhaps he wants a drum he can ride on that will go quack-quack-quack? Or a duck he can play on that will go chug-chug-chug? Or a tractor to swim in his bath and go rub-a-dub-dub?

"But I never heard of playing on a duck; it would have to be a very good-natured duck to stand being played on, surely?

"And how would you ride on a drum?

"As for putting a tractor in the bath, it would certainly have to be a HUGE bath, and even so the sides might get scratched.

"But as Euan is my only nephew, and as he has written to me so politely, I shall have to see what I can do."

So Aunt Bertha put away her knitting, and she took flour and baking powder and nutmeg and cinnamon, she took butter and sugar and eggs and milk and raisins and currants and sultanas and nuts and dates and figs and cherries and candied orange and lemon peel, and she mixed all these things together in a beautiful big bowl with a brown outside and a white inside. She mixed them and she stirred them, round and round, to and fro, up and down, back and forth, a hundred and three times over, with her wishing-spoon.

She put a little old magic silver sixpence into the mixture, and she stirred that in too, a hundred and three times.

Then she poured all the brown, gloopy, spicy mixture into a cake-tin, and baked it in the oven for a hundred and three minutes, until it smelt fruity and spicy and sweet, like Christmas and Easter and birthdays all mixed together.

Aunt Bertha took the cake out of the oven and turned the tin upside down so that the cake slid out on to a plate. Then she let it get cool. Then she turned it the right way up and iced it all over with white sugar mixed with egg-white, and she decorated the cake with a little tractor, and a little drum, and a little duck, all made out of white sugar. And in pink on top of the cake, she wrote the words,

Happy Birthday Evan

and then she wrapped the cake in paper and put it in a box and stuck on a label that said,

THIS WAY UP. PLEASE DO NOT BANG
OR BUMP. KEEP AWAY FROM MICE.

and she wrote Euan's name and address on the side and posted it off at the post office.

The cake reached Euan quite safely and he had it for his birthday-evening tea.

Everybody had a slice, and it was the best cake they had eaten in their whole lives.

And, in Euan's slice, he found the little old magic silver sixpence. There was also a note from Aunt Bertha, a bit brown from having been baked.

Dear Euan, you should put the sixpence under your pillow when you go to bed. It might be a good thing to put the tractor and the duck and the drum under your pillow too. My rheumatism is much better, thank you. Your loving Aunt Bertha.

P S. Then tomorrow, on your birthday, see what you get!

So when Euan went to bed he put the sixpence, the sugar tractor, the sugar duck, and the sugar drum, all under his pillow.

It took him a long time to go to sleep because he was excited.

In the middle of the night he woke up.

The moon was shining like daylight, and his pillow looked like a great snowy hill. Round the hill, chugging slowly along through the snow, came a huge white duck. And down the hill, rolling over and over, going rub-a-dub-dub, came a middle-sized tractor. And over the hill in the moonlight, flying against the blue starry sky, Euan saw a white drum that went quack, quack.

"There's been a muddle somewhere," he thought.

The great white duck chugged up to Euan and

smiled at him with its big smiling yellow beak and gave him a loving look out of its bright, black twinkling eye.

"I'm your friendly duck
Come to bring you luck," it said,
"with the compliments of your Aunt Bertha."

The tractor rolled to a stop in the snow beside Euan and began to play a tune like a musical box.

"Ting-a-ling, ding-a-ding, listen to me
sing
I'm your faithful tractor, sound in limb
and wing."

The drum floated down beside them and perched on a heap of snow.

"Quack quack, I'm your loving drum,
quack, quack, quack
Any time you want a ride, climb upon
my back."

"There's certainly been a muddle," said Euan. "But never mind, let's go."

And he climbed on to the drum and began rolling it along with his feet. This is not at all an easy thing to do, but Euan could do it very well. Then the drum left the ground and started flying through the air, while the duck and the tractor trundled along underneath.

But they had not gone very far when they saw a little man in a fur hat, who was rushing to and fro, to and fro, among a great many heaps of snow. When the man saw Euan he called out,

"Is that a drum you have there? Then you are just in time to take part in the contest."

"What contest?" said Euan. His drum landed in a heap of snow and the tractor and the duck came up and sat beside him.

"We're trying to wake the army," said the man in the fur hat. "They've been asleep for a hundred and three years, but now the enemy are coming. The King is offering half his crown to any drummer who can wake the soldiers."

"Where are they?" said Euan.

He could see two drummers waiting ready with their drums, but he couldn't see any army.

"Under the snow," said the fur-hatted man. "Right, drummer number one, PLAY!"

So the first drummer raised his drumsticks and beat a tattoo on his drum: Rrrrrrrrrrrrrrrr-tat-a-tat-tat-TAT.

Nothing happened, though he banged on his drum so hard that he burst it.

"Right," said the fur-hatted man. "Drummer number two, PLAY!"

The second drummer raised his drumsticks and beat a reveille on his drum: Brrrrrrrrrrr-rum-tum-tiddle-um-tum TUM.

Nothing happened, except that he also broke his drum.

"Right," said the fur-hatted man. "Drummer number three, on your marks, get set, PLAY!"

Euan looked at his three presents, and thought,

"I can't play on the drum, because that's for
riding. And I can't bang on the tractor, because
it sings. So it must be the duck."

The duck nodded, at that, and gave him a
friendly wink of its twinkling black eye. So he
picked up the drumsticks and thumped the duck
on its back. And it went: Brrrrrrrrrrrrrrr-brek-ek-
ek-ex, co-ax, co-ax.

All the heaps of snow began to stir and shuffle.
A hundred and three soldiers sat up and started
shaking off the snow, yawning and rubbing their
eyes. Then they stood up, took bows and arrows
off their backs, bent the bows, and aimed the
arrows.

"Where's the enemy?" said Euan.

"There, coming up the hill."

Sure enough, up the hill came marching an army of a hundred and three Abominable Snowmen. They had snow hats and gloves, their faces were perfectly plain, and the snow was buttoned up to their chins.

But the soldiers, now wide awake, had set fire to all their arrows with matches, and they shot the arrows off, blazing and crackling, and in less time than it takes to tell, the army of Abominable Snowmen had all melted away, sizzle, fizzle, drizzle, grizzle, slup, slurp.

"Well, fancy that," said Euan.

"Many thanks for waking the army," said the fur-hatted man. "I owe you half a crown."

He took off his fur hat. Underneath it was a gold crown, stuck all over with sparkling stones, red and blue and green and yellow and white and pink. He borrowed a sword from one of the soldiers (who were all going back to sleep in the snow again, as fast as they could) and cut the crown in half. Then he gave half to Euan.

"Thank you," said Euan. "But what can I do with half a crown? I can't wear it."

"Half a crown is better than no head. Put it on the tractor's bonnet. It will come in handy some day, I daresay."

So Euan did this, and then he and the tractor and the duck and the drum went on over the snowy hill. This time Euan rode on the duck. It

was very comfortable, like riding on a haycart.

But they had not gone very far when they saw a lot of Romans, pulling on ropes.

"Is that a tractor that you have there?" called the chief Roman. "Then you are just in time to help us, if you will be so kind. For we have got a dragon in our bath, and we can't pull it out."

As well as Romans pulling on the ropes, there were camels and elephants and oxen, horses and mules and a bear and a gorilla and two ostriches, who were more trouble then help, because they kept burying their heads in the snow.

But nothing would shift the dragon. He lay on his back, looking very contented, with his eyes shut, and his feet and his tail sticking out. And the ropes kept breaking and the elephants kept slipping about in the snow. And the hot soapy water was slopping *everywhere*.

"My goodness," said Euan. "Perhaps it will have to be the tractor this time." So he wound up the tractor with its starting-handle, and the tractor rolled up beside the dragon in the Roman bath, and began to sing, very loud and clear, in the dragon's ear.

Ting-a-ling ting, ting, hey-ding-a-ding-a-
ding
Now's the time for dragons to take to the
wing
Breakfast is a-waiting, bacon is
a-sputtering
Eggs are all a-boiling, crumpets are
a-buttering
Tea's in the teapot, cream that the farmer
made
Now's the time for dragons to take a little
marmalade."

At that the dragon opened his eyes, pulled out the
plug with his claw, left the bath, lightning-quick,
with a tremendously loud soapy swoosh, tossing
great slops of water everywhere, and flew away
fast, dripping on everybody as he passed over.

"Well," said the chief Roman, "he could have
done *that* more tidily. But still, thank you, Euan.
As a reward you can have half a Roman holiday."

"What can I do with a half holiday?" said
Euan.

"Put it under the duck's wing. I daresay it'll
come in handy some day."

So Euan put it under the duck's wing and then
he and the tractor and the drum and the duck
went on their way.

The next thing they saw was Euan's Aunt
Bertha, but to start with Euan didn't know it was

his Aunt Bertha, for she was all wound up into a huge tangle of knitting wool as big as a haystack.

The only thing she could say, underneath all the wool, was

"Phoomph! Phoomph!"

"Goodness me," said Euan. "I think there is somebody inside all that wool."

So he tied one end of the wool, which stuck out, to the drum, and then the drum began to spin round and round, round and round and round, round and round, and round and round, a hundred and three times, until it had spun all the wool into a big tidy ball, and there, at the other end, was Aunt Bertha, quite red in the face.

"Poof! It was hot in there," she said. "I thought I'd never get out. First the Abominable Snowmen marched past and unwound all my wool, and then the dragon flew over and tangled it all round me. I certainly am glad you came along, Euan."

"Why, it's my Auntie Birthday," said Euan, and he gave her a hug.

"And are you pleased with your tractor and your drum and your duck?"

"Yes, thank you," said Euan, "but I think there was a bit of a muddle. I wanted a duck that would go in my *bath*. And I wanted a drum that I could *play* on. And I wanted a tractor that I could *ride* on."

At that Aunt Bertha began to laugh like mad.

"Oh what a silly woman I am," she said. "I'm always making mistakes like that. But never mind, we can easily put it right."

So she got out her big brown mixing-bowl with the white inside, and she put Euan into it with the tractor and the duck and the drum, and she took her wishing-spoon with the little shield-shape on the back, and she began to stir.

She stirred and she mixed and she stirred, a hundred and three times, until Euan felt quite dizzy. He seemed to be falling through a white hole, and he shut his eyes tight, tight, tight, and when he opened them again it was morning and he was back in his bed.

Quick as quick he put his hand under his pillow. But all he found there was a crumble of sugar. So then he sat up and looked round the room.

At the end of his bed was a little tractor just his size that he could really ride on. And on the table was a big drum that he could really play on, with two drumsticks. And perched on his windowsill was a beautiful white duck which, the minute he saw it, gave a loud quack! and flew across the room to sit on his quilt, smiling at him with its big yellow beak and its bright black eyes.

On the tractor's bonnet was a half crown, painted in gold.

As for the half Roman holiday, it was nowhere to be seen. But when Euan got to school that morning all his friends stood up and sang, "Happy birthday, Euan." And the teacher said, "As it's Euan's birthday you can all have a half holiday and go home this afternoon."

So all his friends went back with Euan and every single one had a ride on the tractor. And they played on his drum. And that night at bedtime the white duck came and swam in Euan's bath; and it perched on his windowsill all night long.